Something was tickling my hand!

"Look, Roscoe!" Hazel said. "I found this kitty in the pop-up books!"

I opened my eyes. Hazel was holding a tiny kitten.

A real one.

A real, live BLACK CAT!

Never Race a
Runaway Pumpkin

The Roscoe Riley Rules books
by Katherine Applegate

Roscoe Riley Rules #1:
Never Glue Your Friends to Chairs

Roscoe Riley Rules #2:
Never Swipe a Bully's Bear

Roscoe Riley Rules #3:
Don't Swap Your Sweater for a Dog

Roscoe Riley Rules #4:
Never Swim in Applesauce

Roscoe Riley Rules #5:
Don't Tap-Dance on Your Teacher

Roscoe Riley Rules #6:
Never Walk in Shoes that Talk

ROSCOE RILEY

Rules

#7

Never Race a Runaway Pumpkin

Katherine Applegate
illustrated by Brian Biggs

HARPER
An Imprint of HarperCollinsPublishers

Library of Congress Cataloging-in-Publication Data
Applegate, Katherine.
    Never race a runaway pumpkin / Katherine
Applegate ; illustrated by Brian Biggs.—1st ed.
        p.   cm.—(Roscoe Riley rules ; #7)
    Summary: Roscoe is determined to guess the
weight of a giant pumpkin in order to win books
for his school library and candy for himself, but is
overwhelmed by superstitions, especially about a
certain black kitten.
    ISBN 978-0-06-178370-8 (pbk. bdg.)
    ISBN 978-0-06-178372-2 (trade. bdg.)
    [1. Superstition—Fiction.   2. Luck—Fiction.
3. Cats—Fiction.   4. Animals—Infancy—Fiction.
5.   Schools—Fiction.   6.   Humorous   stories.]
I. Biggs, Brian, ill.   II. Title.
PZ7.A6483Nen   2009   2009002089
[Fic]—dc22   CIP
                                                        AC

18 19 20 BRR 20 19 18 17 16 15 14 13 12
❖
First Edition

This book is for
Julia and Jake

Contents

1. Welcome to Time-Out 1

2. Something You Should Know
   Before We Get Started 4

3. Something Else You Should Know
   Before We Get Started 7

4. Buzillions, Katrillions,
   and Other Cool Numbers. 8

5. Ladders and Luck 17

6. How Big Is That Pumpkin
   in the Window? 27

7. Hello, Kitty!. 36

8. Guesstimating 41

9. The Bad-Luck Magnet 48

10. Leaves Dropping. 57

11. And the Winner Is 66

12. Good-Bye from Time-Out. 77

1

Welcome to Time-Out

Hey, friend! Over here, in the time-out corner.

It's me, Roscoe.

I'm pretty sure I only have to stay in time-out for about three more minutes.

That should be plenty of time for me to tell you how I ended up here.

Oops.

1

Mom checked the clock. Turns out I have *seven* more minutes.

I thought seven was supposed to be a lucky number!

My teacher says when you think a number is lucky, that's called a *superstition*.

She says there's no such thing as a lucky number.

And that seven is just like eight and forty-seven and a gazillion.

A plain, old, everyday number.

I used to think lots of things were lucky.

Things like numbers and four-leaf clovers and horseshoes.

I used to think lots of things were *un*lucky, too.

That's sort of how I ended up in time-out.

One thing led to another, and before I knew it, I was being chased down the street by a humongous pumpkin.

And let me tell you, those guys can MOVE.

You've been chased by a giant piece of food before, haven't you?

No?

How about normal-size food?

Not even a little bitty grape?

Oh.

I guess being chased by food doesn't come up all that often.

But I can explain everything.

Have you got seven minutes to spare?

2

Something You Should Know
Before We Get Started

When a kitty rubs her face on your leg, she is just saying hello.

It does not mean she is wondering how you will taste for dinner.

3

Something Else You Should Know Before We Get Started

A pumpkin is a fruit. Not a vegetable.

It's a true fact. I learned it at school.

But take it from me. When the biggest pumpkin in town is about to smush you into a pumpkin-boy pie, you don't really care if it's a fruit or a vegetable.

You just want to get out of its way.

4

Buzillions, Katrillions, and Other Cool Numbers

Sometimes I wish I hadn't gone to the school library last week.

Then I never would have seen the giant pumpkin that got me into so much trouble.

Don't get me wrong. I *love* our school library.

It's the most fun place in my school.

Except maybe for the playground.

Our library has maps. And DVDs. And CDs. And computers.

But most of all, it has tons of books.

My class goes there twice a week for story time.

Our story-time area is shaped like a little pirate ship. On the deck are lots of squishy pillows.

Mr. Page is the library helper who reads to us.

He has the best name for a library guy, I think.

Although *Mr. Shhh* would be good too.

When Mr. Page reads, he wears a black eye patch like a real pirate.

Also, he says, "ARGHH, me hearties!"

Which is Pirate for *Hello, kids!*

This time Mr. Page was wearing an orange eye patch, though.

On account of the book he was going to read to us was about pumpkins.

"Okay, folks," said Mr. Page. "Today's book is called *Pumpkin Power*. It's full of fun facts about pumpkins."

He held up the book. The cover had a picture of a giant pumpkin on it.

"Before we start reading," said Mr. Page, "I want to tell you about an even bigger pumpkin!"

He unrolled a poster.

There was a photo of a boy and a girl on it.

They were each holding a book. And smiling.

And next to them was the most gigantic pumpkin I had ever seen. It looked huge!

It was as tall as my dad.

Almost.

And as big as our car.

Almost.

"That's got to be the world's biggest pumpkin," I cried.

"Actually, giant pumpkins can reach over one thousand six hundred pounds," said Mr. Page. "This one is gigantic, all right. But it's not *that* big."

"Any kind of gigantic is good, if you ask me," I said.

"This poster is from Hilltop Bookstore," Mr. Page said. "They're having a contest. If you guess the weight of the giant pumpkin in their window, you win books for the school library. Enough to fill that giant pumpkin!"

"That's a lot of books!" said Emma.

"You're right, Emma. And we sure could use them," said Mr. Page. "You can make a guess when you visit the bookstore. The winner will be announced at the Fall Festival on Saturday."

"I'll bet that pumpkin weighs two hundred buzillion pounds!" Hassan said.

"Nunh-uh," said Gus. "Seven thousand katrillion pounds, at least."

Emma said, "I'm not sure if buzillion and katrillion are for-real numbers. But googol is a real number, right, Ms. Diz?"

Ms. Diz is our first-grade teacher.

She knows lots of math and spelling.

And also how to wiggle her ears.

"Googol *is* a number, Emma," Ms. Diz said. "A very big number. It has one hundred zeros in it!"

"That pumpkin is for sure a googol

pounds then," I said.

"Children," said Ms. Diz, "maybe we should work on estimating how much things weigh. It could be a wonderful learning opportunity."

When Ms. Diz says *learning opportunity*, she gets very excited.

She is a brand-new teacher, so she likes to try out new ideas on us. Mostly that is a good thing.

But once she let us make marshmallow crispies so we could learn about measuring.

After that Learning Opportunity, she had to send home a letter to all the parents about How to Wash Marshmallow Goo out of Your Child's Hair.

"Kids, I forgot to mention that the contest winner also gets a prize," added

Mr. Page. "Candy. Lots of it. Enough to fill the pumpkin."

"A googol pounds of candy!" said Gus.

He had a goofy smile on his face.

I probably did too.

"ARGHH, me hearties!" said Mr. Page in his pirate voice. "It's time to read!"

He held up the book so we could see the first page.

"'You may think that a pumpkin is a vegetable,'" he read. "'But it's really a fruit, because it has seeds inside of it.'"

Hmm, I thought. It was a very interesting fact.

But not nearly as interesting as the news about the contest.

Mr. Page kept on reading about pumpkins. He talked about giant pumpkins, tiny pumpkins, pumpkin seeds, and pumpkin pie.

My ears tried to pay attention.

But my brain kept thinking how nice it would be to win books for the library.

And candy for me.

5

Ladders
and Luck

When we walked into our classroom the
next morning, there were pumpkins on
Ms. Diz's desk.

A little one and a medium one.

Also there was an apple, a grape, a rock,
and a quarter.

Not only that, Mr. McGeely, the janitor,
was high up on a ladder in a corner of the
room.

He was changing the long lightbulbs.

Pumpkins and lightbulbs!

It was going to be an amazing morning.

"Class, I know a lot of you were interested in the giant pumpkin Mr. Page told us about yesterday," said Ms. Diz. "That's why we're going to learn about how to guess weight today. We call it *estimating*."

Mr. McGeely climbed down from the ladder.

"Replaced all the burned-out lights, Ms. Diz," he said.

"Wonderful," said Ms. Diz. "It's much brighter in here."

It was true. You could see all kinds of things.

On the floor I saw a black crayon and a ball of dust shaped like a kangaroo.

And then I saw a penny!

Right under Mr. McGeely's ladder.

Gus saw it too. He made a dive for it.

Gus was halfway under the ladder before I could grab his shirt.

"Gus, no!" I cried. "You can't go under a ladder! It's seven years of bad luck!"

"No, that's if you break a mirror," Hassan said.

"I think seven years of bad luck is when you step on a crack," Coco said.

"That's for breaking your mom's back," Maya said. "Everybody knows that!"

"*Excuse me!*" Gus interrupted. "We're talking about a free penny here!"

He grabbed for the penny. But I held on tight and slid him back.

"Maybe it's a lucky penny, Roscoe," Gus said.

"But going under the ladder would erase

the lucky and turn it to unlucky," I said.

"Hmm," said Ms. Diz. "I think I see another wonderful learning opportunity."

Two learning opportunities in two days!

No wonder Ms. Diz had such a gigantic smile on her face.

"Children," said Ms. Diz. "Roscoe was worried that if Gus went under a ladder it would be unlucky. But believing that something can cause good luck or bad luck is what we call a *superstition*. Can anyone think of a good reason why walking under a ladder would make bad luck happen?"

"If there was a guy on it painting and the bucket of paint fell on your head," Wyatt said.

"Well, yes," said Ms. Diz. "That would

definitely be bad luck. But—"

Coco raised her hand. "I might have my room painted magenta," she said. "That is what you get when you mix red and blue together."

"Magenta is a very interesting color," said Ms. Diz. "But let's try to stay focused on superstitions. Roscoe, what made you think that going under a ladder would be bad luck?"

"My Uncle Ed told me. He knows lots of good superstitions. And he gave me my lucky four-leaf clover. After I got it, the same day I found an old sucker in my pocket and it was only just a little bit fuzzy. So how lucky was that?"

"Pretty lucky," Ms. Diz agreed.

But I had the feeling she was not a big fan of fuzzy suckers.

Ms. Diz drew a picture of a four-leaf clover and an umbrella on the black-board.

"Some people believe things bring good luck," she said. "And some people believe

doing certain things will bring bad luck.
Like opening an umbrella in the house. Or
breaking a mirror. But superstitions aren't
based on fact, and they aren't real."

"My mom broke a mirror in her purse,"

Maya said. "And then she tripped on my sister's skateboard and broke her toe."

"But that could have happened even if she hadn't broken a mirror," said Ms. Diz.

Emma raised her hand. "My neighbor had a black cat cross in front of her in the park. Then she went to a minigolf place and found a green beetle in her corn dog. She blamed the black cat."

"And I'll bet you told her that didn't make any sense," said Ms. Diz.

"No," said Emma. "I told her not to order the corn dog next time. The very next day she fell in a mud puddle. And after that a skunk got in her kitchen and she had to move out of her house for a week because of the smell."

"Wow," I said. "Black cats really are bad luck!"

"Roscoe," said Ms. Diz, "in many countries, black cats are considered good luck. But the truth is, black cats are not good luck or bad luck. Neither are green kangaroos or purple alligators."

"I know you're the teacher and all," I said, "but I'm pretty sure alligators don't come in purple."

"Let's try this another way," Ms. Diz said. "Emma, do you think the black cat caused your neighbor's problems?"

Emma made a not-sure look.

I know that look. I maybe even invented it.

"How many of you think the black cat caused Emma's neighbor to eat a green beetle and fall in a mud puddle and have a skunk in her house?" Ms. Diz asked.

We all raised our hands.

"How many of you think Maya's mom tripped on a skateboard because she broke a mirror?" Ms. Diz asked.

We all raised our hands again.

"How many of you think I should paint my room magenta?" Coco asked.

Ms. Diz had that I-need-a-nap look she sometimes gets, but usually not until the end of the day.

She took a deep breath. "Maybe we should move on to a different learning opportunity," she said.

6

How Big Is That Pumpkin in the Window?

After school my mom picked up Max, my big brother, and me so we could go to the store to get new jeans.

All my knees had holes again.

My little sister, Hazel, was in her car seat. She was wearing fairy wings, her swimsuit, pajama bottoms, and yellow mittens.

The usual.

"Hazel, your socks don't match," Max said.

"Neither do Roscoe's," she pointed out.

"The red one is my lucky sock," I said. "When I wear it on my right foot, something good always happens."

"Remind me to wash that one of these years," Mom said.

"So what good thing happened today because of your red sock?" Hazel asked.

"Nothing yet," I admitted. "But if Mom will take us to the bookstore, I think something wonderful might happen."

I gave Mom my sweetest smile.

It takes all my smile muscles.

"Mom, can we go to the bookstore after we buy clothes?" I asked. "I need to weigh a giant pumpkin."

Mom looked at me in the rearview mirror. "Could you run that by me again?"

I explained all about the pumpkin and the bookstore and the school winning lots of books.

I kind of forgot to mention the part about me winning a googol pounds of candy.

Mom said yes. Not even "We'll see" or "Maybe some other time, Roscoe."

We drove to a giant store called the Clothes Closet. It has pants and socks and underwear and other stuff that wears out.

It is also probably the most boring place on the planet.

Finally it was time for the bookstore.

Hilltop Bookstore was at the very tip-top of a big hill.

Mom parked the car at the bottom of the hill near a statue of our town founder, Thomas Toadswaddle.

It's a very big statue made of metal.

He is wearing an old-fashioned hat. And holding a porcupine.

Nobody knows why.

I guess he just liked porcupines.

We walked past the statue and up the hill. Max and Hazel and I beat Mom to the bookstore.

There it was at last. The giant pumpkin.

It was beautiful and big and very orange.

It was the size of a baby dinosaur.

Or maybe a teenager elephant.

We made *whoa* and *no way* sounds.

Max whistled. I tried to whistle, but my

whistle has more spit than whistle.

Then Hazel told Mom I was spitting on her.

Which was true. But it doesn't count as real spitting if it's whistle spit. And not on purpose.

When we got inside, the bookstore clerk said, "I saw you checking out our pumpkin. Would you like to guess its weight?"

"You bet!" I said.

"Just write down your guess, and be sure to include your name and phone number," said the bookstore guy, whose name was Dan.

It said so on his name tag.

Sometimes knowing a little about reading comes in very handy.

"I guess fifteen pounds because that's how old Rachel is and she is my favorite babysitter," Hazel said.

"Okay, Hazel," said Mom. "Fifteen pounds it is."

Mom wrote down Hazel's guess for her.

Then Max wrote his.

Mom read the contest rules. "If one of you kids wins, you are all sharing the candy prize," she said. "And you're making it last five years."

"Mommy, can I look at the pop-up books?" Hazel asked.

"Sure," said Mom. "Roscoe, we'll just be over in the children's books. Take your best guess, sweetie."

I walked back and forth past the giant pumpkin.

I looked it up and down.

I knocked on it. I even sniffed it.

Max groaned. "Just write down some number, Roscoe. It's not like you're actually going to win."

Big brothers should come with a set of earplugs.

It is hard to keep your candy-and-books dream alive when they are around.

I touched my lucky red sock for good luck.

Then I closed my eyes and waited to see if the perfect number popped into my brain.

But instead of a number, I thought of a fuzzy caterpillar.

Then I thought of a fuzzy panda bear.

Then I thought of a fuzzy—

Something was tickling my hand!

"Look, Roscoe!" Hazel said. "I found this kitty in the pop-up books!"

I opened my eyes. Hazel was holding a tiny kitten.

A real one.

A real, live BLACK CAT!

7
Hello, Kitty!

I jumped back.

WAY back.

"Hazel!" I cried. "That's a black cat!"

"Well, duh," she said.

"Black cats are bad luck!"

"Roscoe," said Mom, "that's silly."

"Uncle Ed says if a black cat walks in front of you, it's bad luck forever," I said.

"Sweetie, Uncle Ed is my brother and I love him dearly," Mom said. "But he can be a little nutty sometimes. He's the only person I know who owns a pair of lucky underwear."

"We call this kitty No-name," said Dan.

He scratched the kitten behind her ears.

You could hear her purring.

It was an awfully nice sound to be coming from such an unlucky animal.

"We found her outside the front door yesterday morning," Dan said. "We're hoping someone will want to give her a good home."

Hazel held out the kitty. No-name rubbed her head on my arm.

"Somebody stop that thing!" I yelled.

I hid behind my mom.

That's what moms are for, after all.

"Please calm down," Mom said.

I peeked around Mom. "Why was she rubbing on me?" I asked.

"She wanted to see what you'd taste like," said Max.

"She was putting her scent on you," Mom explained.

I sniffed my hand. "I don't smell anything. Except my peanut-butter-and-banana sandwich from lunch."

"You can't smell anything, but she can," said Mom. "And so can other cats. She's trying to say, 'Roscoe belongs to me.'"

"Mom, can we take her home, please?" Hazel begged. *"Pleasepleasepleaseplease?"*

"I'm not sure if Goofy would like that idea," said Mom.

Goofy is our big white silly dog.

I do not actually know what his opinion is on cats.

"But Mom, she's so fuzzy and cute!" Hazel cried.

"I'll think about it," Mom said.

Hazel kissed the kitty's face.

39

"Hazel," I warned, "you're going to have bad-luck germs all over you."

"It's time for us to go, Roscoe," said Mom. "Did you make your guess about the pumpkin's weight?"

The kitten made a little squeaky *mew* sound.

"What was *that*?" I demanded.

"She's putting a curse on you," Max said. But he said it too quietly for Mom to hear him.

I grabbed Mom's arm. "Mom, I really think we should get out of here," I said.

I didn't care about the books for the school anymore.

Or even the candy for my stomach.

Not with that bad-luck kitty around.

8

Guesstimating

The next day at school, we learned more about weighing things.

We learned about Greater Than and Less Than.

We learned that a little pumpkin's weight is greater than a quarter.

We even learned that a medium pumpkin weighs less than Ms. Diz.

The more I thought about weighing stuff, the more I wished I'd taken a guess about the giant pumpkin's weight.

It didn't seem fair that a fuzzy, mewing, purring animal with bad-luck germs was ruining my chance at winning.

All day long I thought about that giant pumpkin.

All day long I thought about that black cat.

Heading home on the school bus, I finally came up with the perfect plan.

I could guess that pumpkin's weight AND keep away from the black cat and her bad luck.

All I had to do was send someone else into the bookstore to write down my guess!

That way, I wouldn't have to go

anywhere near that cat.

I knew just the guy to help me out.

I ran into the house. Dad was doing work stuff in the kitchen.

"How was school, Roscoe?" he asked. He kissed me on top of my head.

I plopped my backpack onto the kitchen table. "We learned all about how to guesstimate weight today."

"Estimate," Dad said. "Cool. How much do you figure I weigh?"

I thought for a minute. "Greater than a mouse. But less than a monster truck."

"Not bad," Dad said.

"I could get a chance for extra practice if you took me back to the bookstore," I said.

Dad raised his eyebrow. "Not the giant pumpkin again?"

"I didn't get to guess last time," I said. "'Cause of the bad-luck kitty."

Dad checked his watch. "Hazel and your mom are at Mommy and Me Music, so you and I have to pick up Max after his

softball practice. I suppose we could stop at the bookstore on the way."

"You're the best dad in the whole entire metropolitan area," I said.

They say that on TV a lot.

"Why, thank you," said Dad.

"Dad, do you believe in superstitions?" I asked.

"Well, I've been known to knock on wood when I'm wishing for good luck. But I know it doesn't really bring me luck."

"Do you have lucky underwear?"

"No. That's your Uncle Ed's department."

"Do you think black cats make you eat green beetles?"

Dad scratched his head. "I'm not sure I'm following you, Roscoe."

"It's like this, Dad," I said. "Would you mind writing down my pumpkin guess while I wait outside the bookstore?"

Dad got an oh-I-get-it face. "Roscoe, your mom told me all about the black cat. If you want to go back to the store, you're going to have to go inside, kitty or no kitty. Black cats do not cause bad luck."

"Not unless they cross your path," I said.

"Roscoe," said Dad firmly, "that's just not true. And the only way you're going to believe it is if you go into that bookstore and see for yourself."

I hate it when parents give you hard choices.

I like my choices nice and easy.

"Okay," I finally said. "I guess I can do that. Probably she won't even be there."

Just to be on the safe side, though, I knocked on a wooden chair extra hard.

The Bad-Luck
Magnet

"Wow!" Dad exclaimed when he saw the pumpkin in the window. "You weren't kidding. That is one big pumpkin!"

"Hello, there!" said Dan. "Back again?"

"My school really needs books," I said.

"And he really likes candy," said Dad with a smile. "Matter of fact, so do I."

"Is No-name around?" I asked.

"I just got here a few minutes ago," said Dan. "But I haven't seen her. Maybe someone decided to take her home."

"My daughter will be disappointed if they did," said Dad. "She spent all of our dinner begging us to add No-name to our family."

No No-name was good news. Finally I could concentrate on more important things.

I thought about the world's biggest pumpkin.

Mr. Page had said it was over one thousand six hundred pounds. He'd shown us a picture of it too.

The bookstore pumpkin was smaller than that. But it was still pretty big.

I thought about the medium-sized

pumpkin at school Ms. Diz had weighed.

It was seventeen pounds.

The bookstore pumpkin weighed a lot more than that one.

Finally I felt ready to take a guess.

I wrote down my number:

964

I put ROSCOE RILEY on my paper.
And also my telephone number.

Then I folded up the paper and put it into the plastic pumpkin that held the other guesses. There were a *lot* of other guesses.

"Good luck," said Dan. "We'll be announcing the winner on Saturday morning during the Fall Festival."

Dad looked at his watch. "We've got a few minutes before we have to pick up Max," he said. "Let's go check out the kids' books section."

That's where Hazel had run into Noname!

"We should probably go get Max," I said quickly.

"We've got plenty of time," Dad said.

I followed him very closely down the aisle.

So far, so good.

No No-name.

We passed the picture book part.

And the pop-up book part.

And the books that have a lot of big words and not enough pictures part.

Just as we passed a tall stack of wizard books, I tripped.

My shoelace was untied.

That happens about twenty times a day.

I bent down to tie my shoe.

But somebody else wanted to help.

No-name!

She leaped out of a bookshelf and grabbed my shoelace.

"It's her, Dad!" I cried.

I could feel the bad luck rubbing off on me.

"Just relax," said Dad. "She's only play-ing. Kittens love string."

I stood statue still.

"Dad," I said in a trembly voice, "I will have to burn this shoe. It is totally covered with unluckiness."

No-name rubbed on me. Right on my lucky red sock.

"Great," I said. "Now I have bad-luck cat stink all over my red sock."

Dad grinned. "I think she likes you."

"Dad," I said. "We have to get out of here. If she walks in front of us, we are cursed forever. Or for seven years. I'm not exactly sure which."

Gently Dad pulled the shoelace from No-name's little claws. Then he picked her up.

"*Dad!*" I cried. "What is wrong with you?"

"I'm just holding her," he said. "It's not like she's crossing my path."

No-name made that rumbly purring noise again.

She sounded like she'd swallowed a little toy engine.

It was a good sound. But I knew it was just a sneaky cat trick.

She wanted me to think she was cute so she could cross my path and ruin my life.

"Please can we go now? She's already unlucked my lucky sock."

"All right," Dad said.

I dashed ahead of him down the aisle.

I guess No-name thought I wanted to play catch-the-boy.

She jumped right out of Dad's arms.

And she ran right after me and my shoelace.

"Help!" I cried. "I'm being chased by
bad luck!"

10

Leaves Dropping

I spun around and ran toward the back of the bookstore.

I saw an open doorway and flew inside.

I was in a tiny office. A lady sat at a desk, talking on the phone.

She had a tissue in her hand and a red nose.

She looked very surprised to see me.

"Sweetie, you're not supposed to be in here," she said. "This is the office. Are you lost?"

"No, I'm just looking," I said, because that's what my mom always says to store helpers.

"Well, just let me finish up this call, and I'll see if I can help you," she said.

I peeked out the door.

No-name was waiting for me.

Her tail swished back and forth like windshield wipers.

She was plotting how to cross my path.

I could see it in her shiny green eyes.

The office lady sneezed.

"Yes, I know," she said into the phone. "She's a darling kitten, but I'm so allergic. I'm sure someone will take her home on Saturday."

I heard footsteps. Dad poked his head in the door.

"Roscoe," he said. "That cat is not going to give you bad luck. But *I* will, if you don't start listening to reason."

"Can I help you, sir?" the lady asked.

"Just collecting my son," Dad said.

He took my hand and pulled me out of the office.

No-name sat in the aisle, swishing her tail and waiting for her chance to curse me.

"Run, Dad," I yelled.

I rushed toward the exit as fast as I could.

No-name rushed after me.

Just as I reached the front door, it swung open.

A boy carrying a strawberry milkshake came in.

I crashed into him.

He crashed into me.

The strawberry milkshake crashed into my T-shirt.

No-name took one look at the mess and ran the other way.

I was pink. And milky.

But I'd outsmarted that bad-luck kitty.

● ● ●

"Roscoe, what happened to your white T-shirt?" Mom asked when we got home.

"A strawberry milkshake ran into me," I said.

"We stopped by the bookstore so Roscoe could take a guess on the megapumpkin," Dad said. "I met No-name, by the way, Hazel. She is a very cute kitty. Although Roscoe might not agree with me."

"Can we have her, Dad? Can we, *please*?" Hazel begged. "I could dress her in my doll clothes and name her Bitsy Boo."

"Bitsy Boo? You've got to be kidding!" Max

laughed. "How about Rocky?"

Hazel shook her head. "Nope. She's a girl and she needs a girl name."

"Well, call her what you want. But you can't dress her in doll clothes," Max said. "Right, Mom?"

"Right," said Mom. "Cats generally aren't in favor of playing dress-up."

"Everybody," I said loudly, "we can't get No-name."

"We're just considering the idea," Dad said. "We haven't made a final decision."

"But you *can't* get her," I said.

"Roscoe, I told you that black cats are not bad luck," Mom said.

I took a big breath. "We can't get her because I heard the lady in the bookstore office say someone was for sure already taking her home on Saturday. I was sort of eavesdropping."

Hazel's eyes got wide. "Mommy, what's leaves dropping?" she asked.

"Listening to a conversation you're not supposed to be listening to," said Mom.

"Are you sure about this, Roscoe?" Dad asked.

"Positive," I said.

At least I was pretty sure that's what the lady said.

Maybe not exactly sure.

But kind of sure.

And besides, I didn't want my family to have bad luck move in with them.

Shoelace-grabbing, cute-purring, big-eye-blinking bad luck.

Hazel's eyes got wet with tears.

"But I wanted her to be *my* kitty!" she sobbed.

"I'm sorry, sweetheart," said Mom. "If we decide to get a kitty, there are lots of sweet cats at the animal shelter."

Goofy trotted over to Hazel. He tried to lick her tears.

She blew her nose on Mom's shirt.

She looked so sad.

"Hazel," I said. "Maybe . . ."

"Maybe what?" Hazel asked, sniffling loudly.

"Um, never mind," I said.

I was not exactly sure what I was going to say.

Maybe I was going to say that maybe I wasn't really sure about No-name being taken already.

Maybe.

But I guess I'll never know, because I didn't say it.

11

And the Winner Is...

Saturday morning the town square was full of people.

Main Street was closed for the Fall Festival. No cars could go there, but people could.

I saw dunking for apples. And carved pumpkins. There was even a scarecrow competition.

But the giant pumpkin was the big attraction.

Somehow those bookstore guys had managed to put it on a big wooden cart. Like a pumpkin wagon.

It sat in the middle of the street at the very top of the hill.

Next to the pumpkin were two giant sacks.

"Look at all that, Hazel," I said. "Probably one is full of books for the school. And one is full of candy for us!"

But she didn't answer.

She was still sad about No-name, I guess.

She hadn't even eaten her pancakes this morning.

Even though Dad had made them in the shape of an *H*.

A huge crowd had gathered for the pumpkin-winner announcement. We stood behind lots of other people.

I couldn't see much.

Just the top of Dan the bookstore guy's head. And half of the giant pumpkin.

Dan picked up a microphone.

It made a screechy sound.

"Folks," he said, "Hilltop Bookstore is proud to announce the winner of our Guess the Weight of the Giant Pumpkin Contest!"

"Mom, can I go see the pumpkin close-up?" I asked.

"Sure," Mom said. "Take Hazel with you."

Hazel and I made our way to the front of the crowd.

Near Dan's feet, I noticed a cardboard box.

It had holes in it.

Someone had drawn orange and yellow leaves on the sides of the box.

On the front of the box was a sign that said:

Please FALL for me!
No-name the Kitten
needs a loving home.

Uh-oh, I thought.

"The winner of our contest will win books for their school library," said Dan. "Enough to fill this giant pumpkin!"

The box moved, just a little.

"Roscoe, what's in that box?" Hazel asked. "It keeps wiggling."

"Today's winner guessed exactly the right weight," Dan said.

The box jiggled again.

Hazel yanked on my shirt. "What's that sign on the box say, Roscoe?" she asked.

Dan opened up a piece of paper.

"With the only correct guess of nine hundred sixty-four pounds, the winner is . . . ROSCOE RILEY!" Dan yelled.

"That's me!" I cried. "I'm Roscoe Riley!"

"Roscoe, come on up here, my friend, and take a bow," said Dan.

I ran up to Dan. Then I bowed and waved to the crowd.

Dan shook my hand, and a lady from the local newspaper took a picture of me.

Mom and Dad and Max smiled and waved.

Hazel crept closer to the box.

She poked at the top of it.

"Hazel, no!" I whispered.

But it was too late.

The box popped open. No-name leaped out.

She gave a little meow. Then she took a big leap.

Right for my shoelace.

She grabbed my lace with her kitty claws.

I could feel the bad luck pouring over me.

I fell backward. Right into the pumpkin cart.

The giant pumpkin rocked back and forth.

"Mommy! Daddy! It's the kitty!" Hazel yelled.

Slowly the pumpkin rolled off the cart.

It started down the hill. Just like a giant

piece of fruit going for a nice stroll.

"Look out, folks!" Dan yelled. "Runaway pumpkin!" The giant pumpkin was escaping, and it was all my fault.

"Don't worry, Dan!" I cried. "I'll stop it!"

The pumpkin rolled a little faster. Then faster still.

Most people moved out of its way.

But some ran after the pumpkin with me.

Kids, mostly.

It's not all that often you get to chase giant fruit.

I ran my fastest.

No-name ran beside me.

You could tell she thought chase-the-boy-chasing-the-pumpkin was a wonderful new game.

The pumpkin picked up steam, but so did I.

I was behind it!

I was chasing it!

I was ahead of it!

It was chasing ME!

I was almost to the bottom of the hill.

The statue of Thomas Toadswaddle stood just a few feet away.

I didn't want to get between Thomas and 964 pounds of pumpkin.

So I did what any sensible kid would do.

I jumped out of the way.

No-name jumped too.

Right onto my head.

Which I believe is even worse luck than crossing your path.

The giant pumpkin smashed right into

Thomas and his porcupine.
The pumpkin split right in two.

Pumpkin guts were everywhere.

Orange and slimy and full of seeds and pumpkin juice.

It smelled just like Halloween.

No-name jumped off my head.

She circled around me, purring happily.

That kitty crossed my path big-time.

The crowd was running toward us to see if we were okay.

I was. And so was No-name.

The pumpkin not so much.

12

Good-Bye
from Time-Out

So that's how I ended up here in time-out.

When Mom and Dad found out I had sort of exaggerated about No-name finding a home, they were not very happy.

They said I should have told them *exactly* what I'd overheard in the bookstore office.

Not *kind of* what I'd heard.

They also said black kitties are absolutely, positively NOT bad luck.

Mom and Dad made me promise to talk to them if I have any more superstitions.

And not to Uncle Ed.

They also made me promise not to chase any more runaway fruit.

Or vegetables.

The bookstore made good use of all the pumpkin guts.

I guess a pumpkin really is a fruit. Because that thing was full of seeds.

Dan roasted the seeds and gave them away to customers.

He made about a googol pumpkin pies too.

And guess what else?

No-name is our kitty now.

Except that she isn't called No-name anymore.

Her name is Bitsy Boo now.

We haven't had any bad luck since we brought her home.

I have to admit I like her swishing tail and her blinking eyes and her fluffy black kitten fur.

But you know what I like best of all?

Hear that sound?

Kind of like the world's tiniest motorcycle?

Time-out goes a lot faster when someone's purring in your lap.

10 USEFUL THINGS I LEARNED AT THE BOOKSTORE

by Me, Roscoe Riley

1. Do not ask the bookstore lady to come to your house and read you a bedtime story. She has other plans.

2. There will never be enough books about dinosaurs, pirates, or boogers.

3. First graders are not Young Adults.

4. Say "Store Manager." Not "Boss of the Books."

5. If you knock over the giant stack of Harry Potters, be sure to say sorry to the bookstore lady. Then she will say, "That's okay, sweetheart."

6. If you pop a pop-up book so much that it stops popping, be sure to say you're *extra* sorry to the bookstore lady. Then she will say, "That's okay." She will also ask, "Who is keeping an eye on you, sweetheart?"

7. The bookstore manager cannot call your favorite author and ask why it is taking so long for her to write another book.

8. Do not climb the rolling ladder that goes to the tip-top bookshelf. Especially when you are holding a Junie B. Jones in one hand and a Captain Underpants in the other.

9. During story time, do not yell out the ending of a story. The other kids will not exactly appreciate it.

10. There is a rule called Do Not Write in the Book Unless You Are Pretty Sure Your Mom Is Going to Buy It.

Discover more

ROSCOE RILEY
Rules!

Roscoe Riley Rules #1:
Never Glue Your Friends to Chairs

If the kids can't sit still for the class performance, Roscoe's teacher could be in big trouble. Fortunately Roscoe has a plan to save her—a super-mega-gonzo plan! What could go wrong?

Roscoe Riley Rules #2:
Never Swipe a Bully's Bear

When Roscoe's stuffed pig goes missing, he

is convinced that Wyatt, the class bully, is responsible. When Roscoe finds out where Wyatt keeps his teddy bear, he decides to give that old bully a taste of his own medicine. That will fix everything. Won't it?

Roscoe Riley Rules #3:
Don't Swap Your Sweater for a Dog

It seems like everyone has an award of some kind. Except Roscoe. But a pet-trick contest is coming up, and first prize is a big, shiny trophy. Roscoe really wants that trophy—would he even borrow someone else's dog to win?

Roscoe Riley Rules #4:
Never Swim in Applesauce

Roscoe wants to be on his best behavior for a class trip to the apple orchard. But no matter how hard he tries, he still ends up in a very sticky situation!

Roscoe Riley Rules #5:
Don't Tap-Dance on Your Teacher

Tap shoes make the best noise ever! But tap-*dancing*? The big boys say that's just for girls. Roscoe promised to tap in the school talent show. When the teasing starts, will he keep his word?

Roscoe Riley Rules #6:
Never Walk in Shoes That Talk

Roscoe's friend Gus wants a pair of cool new shoes. But Gus's parents won't buy them until his old, boring ones are worn out—and that could take forever. Luckily if there's one thing Roscoe is good at, it's destroying things. . . .

Katherine Applegate is not, has never been, and most likely never will be the coolest kid in school. She will never be accused of setting fashion trends either, and that's just fine with her. Her husband, two kids, dogs, guinea pigs, and cat like her just the way she is. She is the author of many books for children and lives in California.

Join Roscoe on the rest of his way cool misadventures

Don't miss the other books in this **HILARIOUS** series by bestselling author Katherine Applegate

ROSCOE RILEY Rules #1

Never Glue Your Friends to Chairs

Katherine Applegate
illustrated by Brian Biggs

ROSCOE RILEY Rules #2

Never Swipe a Bully's Bear

Katherine Applegate
illustrated by Brian Biggs

ROSCOE RILEY Rules #3

Don't Swap Your Sweater for a Dog

Katherine Applegate
illustrated by Brian Biggs

ROSCOE RILEY Rules #4

Never Swim in Applesauce

Katherine Applegate
illustrated by Brian Biggs

ROSCOE RILEY Rules #5

Don't Tap-Dance on Your Teacher

Katherine Applegate
illustrated by Brian Biggs

ROSCOE RILEY Rules #6

Never Walk in Shoes that Talk

Katherine Applegate
illustrated by Brian Biggs

HARPER
An Imprint of HarperCollins*Publishers*

www.harpercollinschildrens.com